Brave Bear

Kathy Mallat

Walker & Company
New York

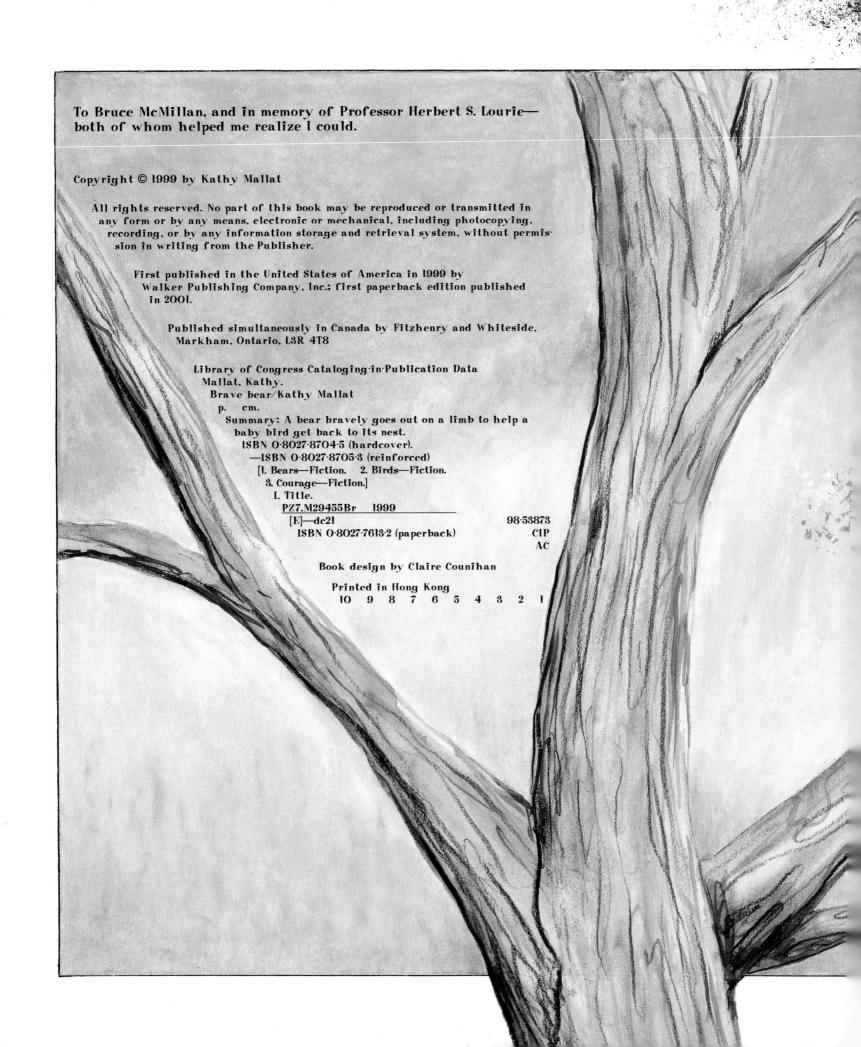

To Bruce McMillan, and in memory of Professor Herbert S. Lourie—
both of whom helped me realize I could.

Copyright © 1999 by Kathy Mallat

First published in the United States of America in 1999 by
Walker Publishing Company, Inc.; first paperback edition published
in 2001.

Published simultaneously in Canada by Fitzhenry and Whiteside,
Markham, Ontario, L3R 4T8

Library of Congress Cataloging-in-Publication Data
Mallat, Kathy.
  Brave bear/Kathy Mallat
  p.   cm.
  Summary: A bear bravely goes out on a limb to help a
  baby bird get back to its nest.
  ISBN 0-8027-8704-5 (hardcover).
    —ISBN 0-8027-8705-3 (reinforced)
  [1. Bears—Fiction.   2. Birds—Fiction.
  3. Courage—Fiction.]
    I. Title.
    PZ7.M29455Br   1999
    [E]—dc21   98-53873
    ISBN 0-8027-7613-2 (paperback)   CIP
                                                AC

Book design by Claire Counihan

Printed in Hong Kong
10 9 8 7 6 5 4 3 2 1

Are you all right?

Can I help you?

Where?

Over there?

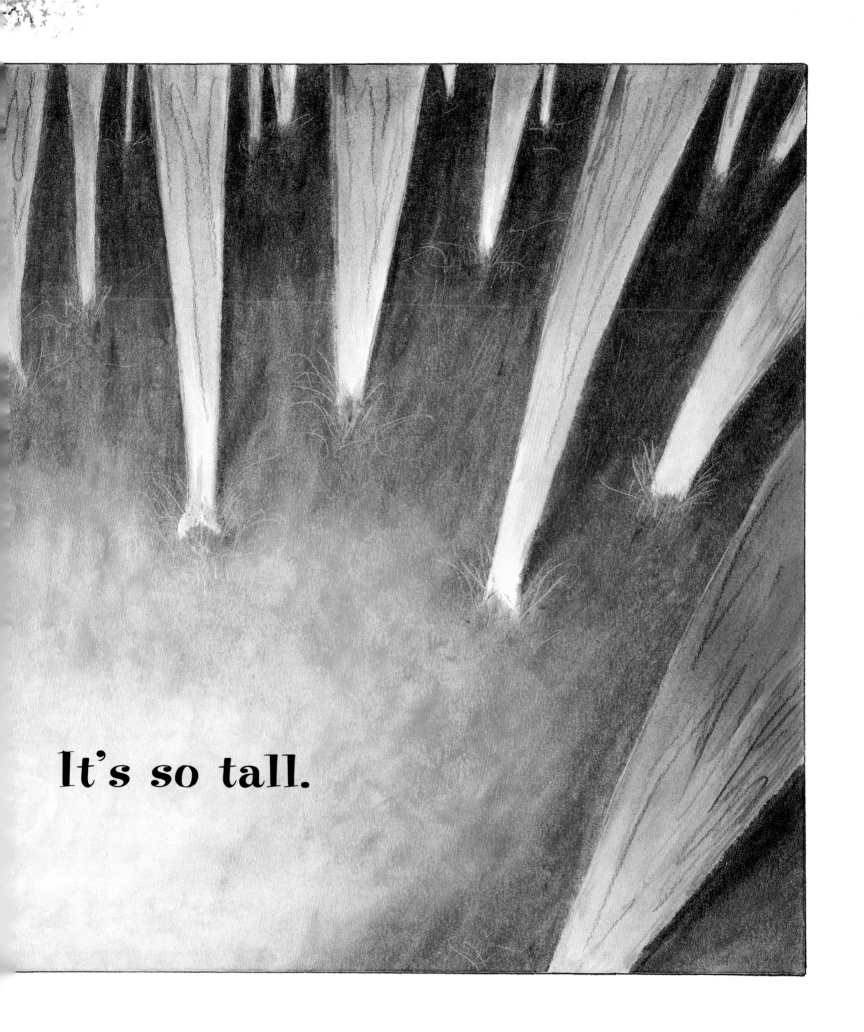

It's so tall.

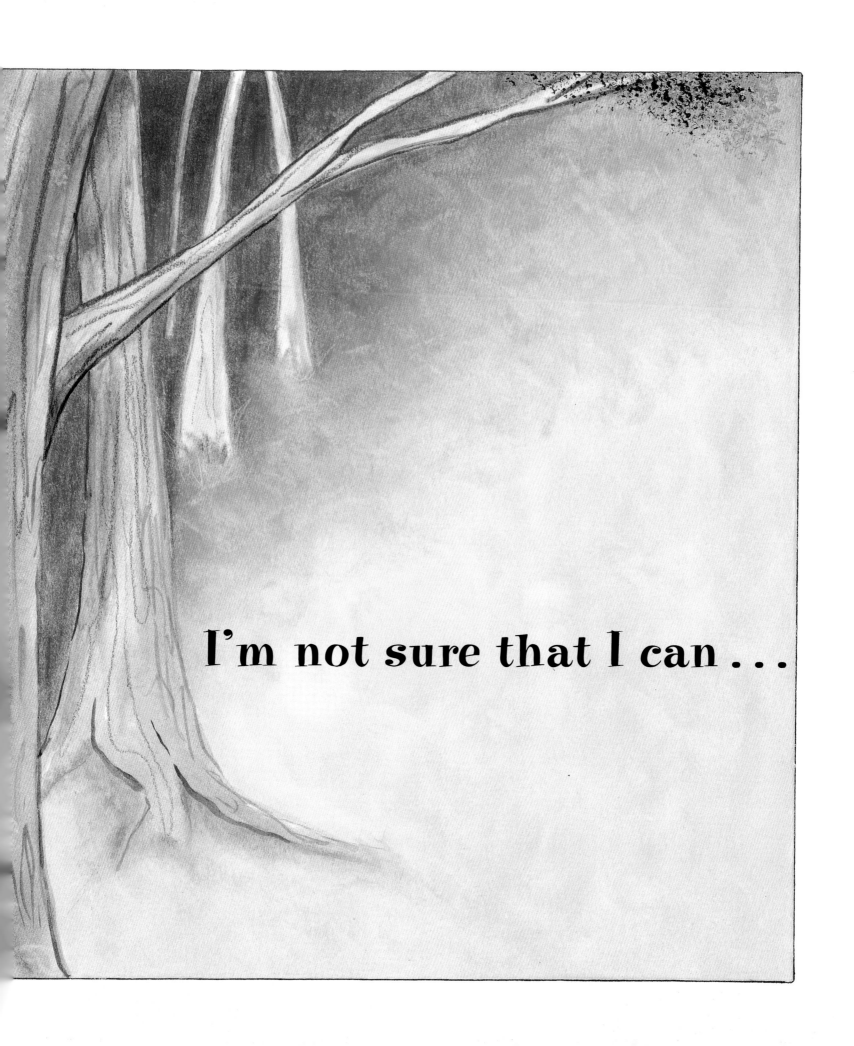

I'm not sure that I can . . .

but I'll try.

I'm scared.

I need help.

Thanks.

We're almost there.

I'm sure I can.

I did.